Hans Christian Andersen

The Princess and the Pea

and other fairy tales

Miles
Kelly

First published in 2015 by Miles Kelly Publishing Ltd
Harding's Barn, Bardfield End Green, Thaxted, Essex, CM6 3PX, UK

2 4 6 8 10 9 7 5 3 1

Publishing Director Belinda Gallagher
Creative Director Jo Cowan
Editorial Director Rosie Neave
Editor Amy Johnson
Designers Rob Hale, Joe Jones
Production Manager Elizabeth Collins
Reprographics Stephan Davis, Jennifer Cozens, Thom Allaway

ISBN 978-1-78209-773-0

Printed in China

British Library Cataloguing-in-Publication Data
A catalogue record for this book is available from the British Library

ACKNOWLEDGEMENTS
The publishers would like to thank the following artists who have contributed to this book:

Front cover: Rosie Butcher (The Bright Agency)

Inside illustrations:
The Princess and the Pea Claudia Venturini (Plum Pudding Illustration Agency)
The Tinder Box Martina Peluso (Advocate-art)
The Flying Trunk Christine Battuz (Advocate-art)
The Buckwheat Kristina Swarner (The Bright Agency)

Border illustrations: Louise Ellis (The Bright Agency)

Made with paper from a sustainable forest

www.mileskelly.net
info@mileskelly.net

Contents

The Princess and the Pea

O nce upon a time there was a prince who wanted to marry a princess – but she had to be a *real* princess.

So he set off to find one. The prince journeyed all over the world, visiting

countries near and far, and he met many princesses on his travels. But not one of them would do. Out of all the hundreds of pretty (and plain), clever (and foolish), entertaining (and boring), good-hearted (and mean-natured) princesses that the prince met, he didn't think any of them had that special something that made them a real princess.

After years of searching, the prince finally gave up hope. He headed home again, his heart filled with great sadness, for he wished so much to have a real princess to love.

One evening, the prince was sitting with his father and mother by the fire in his castle, while a terrible storm raged outside. Towering black clouds blotted out the stars.

Howling gusts of wind tore at the castle turrets. Torrents of rain came crashing onto the battlements. Daggers of lightning slashed through the sky and ear-splitting thunder exploded overhead. It was truly terrifying!

Suddenly, in the midst of the din, the prince heard a steady banging. Whatever could it be? It sounded very much like someone knocking at the castle door, but who would brave being outside in such terrible weather?

The prince and his parents listened carefully… Yes, there it was again – it was definitely someone knocking at the castle door. Very puzzled – and a little worried – the old king went to answer it.

To his great amazement, a young woman was standing there. And good gracious, what a sight she looked! The wind had wound her hair into tangles and the rain had soaked her through – she looked as though she had been tumbled about in a whirlpool and then forced to stand under a waterfall.

As the old king ushered the bedraggled girl inside, the water ran from her hair and clothes, and from the end of her nose. The old queen arrived in the hall to find her shivering with drips trickling into the toes of her shoes and running out again at the heels.

And yet, even though the girl didn't look royal, she insisted that she was a princess.

'Hmm,' thought the old queen, raising an eyebrow. 'We'll soon find that out.' But she said nothing at all. Instead, she hurried off to the finest guest room and stripped all the bedding off the bed – she even heaved the huge mattress off as well.

Then she placed a single pea, very carefully, on top of the bare bed frame, right in the middle. Finally, she replaced the mattress and called for servants to layer another nineteen mattresses on top – the

thickest that could be found – and then pile twenty duckfeather quilts on top of that.

Meanwhile, the princess had been given towels and hot soup and was recovering by the fire. When the old queen was satisfied that everything was ready, the princess was shown to the guest room. She didn't bat an eyelid at the mountainous bed that stood before her. She just said a very heartfelt thank you and shut the door.

The next morning, the first thing the old queen said to the princess was to enquire politely if she had slept well enough.

"Oh dreadfully, I am afraid," sighed the princess. "I have hardly closed my eyes all night. Heaven only knows what was in my bed, but I was lying on something hard. I am bruised black and blue all over!"

Then the royal family knew that the girl truly was a real princess, for she had felt the tiny pea through the twenty mattresses and twenty quilts. Only a *real* princess could possibly be that sensitive.

The prince was overjoyed – he had found the right girl at last! The couple were soon married, and indeed lived happily ever after.

As for the pea, well, it was put on display in a museum, where you can still see it today (if no one has stolen it by now).

The Tinder Box

A soldier was on his way home from war when he met an old witch who said, "You look very brave! I am sure you deserve lots of money – and I know of a way you can get it. See that large tree with

the hole in its trunk? It is hollow inside. Tie a rope around the trunk and let it tumble inside. Then climb through the hole.

"You will find yourself in a hall with three doors. Go into the first room and there will be a chest on the floor. On the chest will be a dog, with eyes as large as teacups. Don't be afraid. I will give you my blue checked apron – spread it on the floor, then put the dog on it and he won't hurt you. The chest will be full of copper coins – you can take them all.

"However, if you would rather have silver, go into the second room. Here you will find another chest with a dog on it that has eyes as big as mill-wheels. Put the dog on my apron, open the chest and take the silver.

"But if you like gold best, go into the third room. There will be a dog there whose eyes are as big as castle turrets. Take him off the chest and put him on my apron. Then you can take as much gold as you like.

"In return, all I want is a tinder box that's in there," said the witch. "You know – the sort of box that people keep bits of flint in, for sparking up a fire."

"Very well," said the soldier.

So the witch gave him her blue checked apron and the soldier went inside the tree.

Everything was just as the witch had said. The first dog was terrifying! But he followed the witch's instructions and the dog didn't hurt him. The soldier filled his pockets and

knapsack with copper. But in the second
room, he threw away the copper coins and
filled his pockets and knapsack with silver
instead. In the third room, he threw away the
silver and filled his pockets, knapsack, cap and
boots with gold! Then he found the tinder

box and clambered back out of the tree.

"Give me the tinder box," said the witch.

"Tell me why you want it," said the soldier cleverly, "or I will cut off your head."

The witch turned red with fury. "No," she said, and began to mutter a magic spell.

At once, the soldier drew his sword and cut off her head. Then he went to the nearest town, where he stayed at the best inn – for now he had plenty of money. Everyone saw that the soldier was rich and wanted to get to know him. And as he talked to people, he came to hear of the king's beautiful daughter.

"No one is allowed to see her," one of his new friends explained. "A wise woman once told the king that the princess would marry a

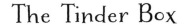

common soldier. The king was so horrified that he shut the princess away in the castle."

'I would like very much to see the princess,' thought the soldier. Then he remembered the witch's tinder box. He waited till midnight, then took a piece of flint out of the tinder box and struck it.

The dog with eyes as big as teacups appeared. "What are your orders, O master?"

"Er… I would like to see the princess," said the astonished soldier.

The dog disappeared and returned in a flash, with the sleeping princess on his back. She looked so lovely that the soldier could not help kissing her, before the dog took her back.

In the morning, the princess told the king

and queen that she had had a very strange dream. A dog had taken her to a soldier, who had kissed her! Next night, the queen set her oldest lady-in-waiting to keep watch.

The soldier longed to see the princess once more, so he struck the flint again, and the dog with eyes as big as teacups appeared as before. When ordered, the dog fetched the princess. But the lady-in-waiting followed and marked the door of the soldier's inn with a chalk cross. She went home and the dog presently returned the princess. But when the dog saw the cross, he put one on every other door too!

The next night, the queen filled a little bag with buckwheat flour, and cut a tiny hole in it. She then tied it round the princess's neck.

During the night, the dog with eyes like teacups came and carried off the princess to the soldier – who had fallen deeply in love with her. But the dog did not notice the flour running out of the bag all the way to the soldier's window. So in the morning, the king and queen found out where their daughter had been, and the soldier was put in prison.

In his cell, the soldier stood on tiptoe and peeped out through the little barred window.

He called to a passing shoemaker's boy: "Run to the best inn in town and fetch my tinder box, and I will give you five gold coins."

So the shoemaker's boy did, double-quick.

Then the soldier struck the flint in the tinder box one… two… three times – and there stood all the dogs: the one with eyes as big as teacups, the one with eyes as large as mill-wheels, and the third, whose eyes were like castle turrets. They leapt together at the prison wall and burst through it as if it were paper. The soldier was free! When all the townspeople saw him appear with his magical servants, they clapped and cheered.

"Hooray!" they cried. "What a hero! You should marry the beautiful princess!"

The king and queen were forced to agree – otherwise the people would have rioted. So the soldier married the beautiful princess and became a prince. Everyone celebrated joyfully, while the dogs were guests of honour at the wedding feast and sat staring with their massive eyes.

The Flying Trunk

Long ago and far away, there was a merchant who was so rich that he could have paved the whole town with gold – and still have bags more left over. Of course, he wasn't silly enough to do such a thing. In fact,

he used his money very wisely, so he made bags more. By the time the merchant died, he was an enormously wealthy man. All his heaps of money passed to his son – who wasted it quicker than you could say 'down the drainpipe.'

He used notes to make paper aeroplanes, and skimmed gold coins into the sea – and very soon the fortune was all gone. Then he found his friends were gone too – for they were all nasty people who had only liked him because he was rich. In fact, one of them sent him an old trunk with a message: Pack up!

"Yes, pack up," the young man said, "that would be a good idea, if I had anything left to pack!" So he just climbed into the trunk himself and sat, fiddling with the lock.

To his great amazement, as he pressed on it, away flew the trunk right up into the clouds! Off he soared, all the way to the land of Turkey. Then he pressed the lock once more and the trunk came gently down to earth.

The young man was delighted with the magic trunk, which had cheered him up a great deal. He hid it carefully in a wood, covering it with branches and leaves, and then made his way to a nearby town. He wandered around, exploring, until he came to a magnificent castle. He asked a passerby who lived there. "The king's daughter," the woman replied. "She is very beautiful."

"Thank you," said the young man. He walked around for a while longer, thinking about the princess. He decided he wanted to meet her, and so he hurried back to the trunk, and flew it up to the roof of the castle. He landed there, then crept through a window into the princess's bedroom.

She lay there, asleep, and she was so beautiful that he couldn't take his eyes off her. As he stood there, the princess woke up and was very frightened. So the young man told her a fib – he said he was an angel, who had come down from heaven to see her.

The princess was delighted at this. The young man entertained her by telling stories, and she found him very charming.

When he asked her to marry him, she said yes at once. "But you must come on Saturday," she said, "for then my father and mother are coming to tea. They will be very pleased when they hear I am going to marry an angel. Make sure you think of some more wonderful stories, for my parents like to hear stories better than anything. My mother likes tales that teach a lesson, but my father likes funny stories that make him laugh."

"Very well," the young man replied, and said goodbye. But before he went, the princess gave him a gift – a sword studded with gold coins.

The young man then flew straight to the town, where he exchanged the sword for some fine new clothes which would be fit for meeting the king and queen. Then he went back to the wood where he could sit alone and think, and make up a story for Saturday.

When the day finally came, he flew back to the castle. There, the princess, king, queen – and in fact the whole court – were waiting for the angel. They welcomed him most politely, and then the queen said: "Will you tell us a story that teaches us something?"

"But one that makes us laugh too," added the king.

"Certainly," he replied, and so he began. "My story is called 'The Last Laugh'. There was once a princess who met a man who said he was an angel. He then made the king and queen believe that he was an angel too."

The king began to chuckle. "What a silly family," he said. "How could they fall for something like that?"

The young man continued, "So when the angel asked for the princess's hand in marriage, the answer was yes. After the wedding, the princess and her parents found out that the man didn't have wings and wasn't an angel after all. But in fact, he could

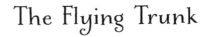

actually fly. For he had a magic trunk which he could sit in and soar through the air. So the man had the last laugh, for they thought he was as good as an angel after all.

"And the moral of this story is: never believe what people tell you, unless you have seen proof."

Then the queen clapped her hands and the king shouted "Bravo!" and the courtiers all murmured to each other in delight.

Only the princess sat in silence, thinking.

Still, the wedding day was fixed for later that week. The evening before, a great festival was held in the town so everyone could celebrate. The king ordered that cakes were to be given out among the people, and bands played music outdoors so everyone could dance in the streets. Jugglers and acrobats performed among the crowds, and everyone thought it was a very jolly affair.

'I will give them another treat,' thought the merchant's son. So he went and bought rockets and Catherine wheels and every sort of firework that you can think of. He packed them in his trunk and flew up into the air.

What a whizzing and popping they made as they burst open like flowers! And how amazed everyone was to see him in the sky!

But alas, a spark from one of the fireworks landed on the trunk and set it alight. The merchant's son only just made it back down to the ground before the smouldering object

31

burst into flames and burned away to ashes.

So the merchant's son could not fly any more, nor go to meet his bride. But perhaps that was just as well. She had realized that she had been tricked and was waiting to kick him out of the kingdom, for of course she didn't want to marry a liar – flying trunk or no flying trunk.

Today, the merchant's son wanders through the world making a living by telling fairy tales, but none of them are as entertaining as his own story.

The Buckwheat

From its name, buckwheat sounds as if it should be a cereal, like wheat or rye. But it is not a grain. It is not even a grass. It is in fact a flowering wild plant with seeds that can be used in cooking or ground down to make flour.

If you come across a field of buckwheat after there has been a violent thunderstorm, very often it looks blackened and burned, as if it has been briefly set on fire. People who live in the countryside say that it gets singed in the lightning. But sparrows say that the lightning strikes it down on purpose.

The sparrows told me once that they heard the real reason why from a willow tree. He is a very old and distinguished willow tree, and completely to be trusted – even if he does look rather crippled by age. His trunk has split and brambles and grass have taken root there. The tree stoops forward slightly and the branches hang quite down to the ground,

just like wispy strands of green hair.

Today in the surrounding fields different types of corn grow there – not only rye and barley but also oats. The oats are the prettiest; when the grains are ripe they look like little golden canary-birds sitting on a bough. But all the corn looks beautiful, standing in the sunshine. When the ears are heavy with grain they bend and nod humbly.

Once, long ago, a field of buckwheat grew there too, exactly opposite the old willow tree. But the buckwheat did not bend like the grain. Instead, it stood up straight and stiff, holding its head up proudly.

"I am just as important as all the corn," one of the buckwheat plants remarked boastfully to the willow tree one day, "and I must say, I am *much* more beautiful! My flowers are as pretty as apple blossom. It's quite a delight to look at me and my family. You must agree, old willow tree. Do you know of any plant prettier than we are?"

At that moment a breeze blew around the willow tree. He nodded his head and dipped his branches as if to say, 'Indeed I do.'

The buckwheat wasn't put off at all. In fact, the plant spread herself out even wider with pride. "Stupid tree!" she scoffed rudely. "He's so old and has been there so long that he's got grass sprouting out of his body!"

Time went by and one night, a terrible storm blew up. The wind howled and plucked at the plants with strong fingers. The rain lashed down on them. All the plants in the cornfields hurried to fold up their leaves and bow their heads, to try to avoid harm. But the buckwheat plants refused to do so. They simply stood up straighter than ever.

"Bow down as we do," urged the other wildflowers, worriedly.

"Why should we?" replied the buckwheat.

"Bow down as we do," cried the ears of corn. "The angel of the storm is coming, and his wings spread from the sky above to the earth down below. He will cut you in half before you can even cry out."

"There's nothing that can make us bow down," stated the buckwheat brazenly. "We will not bow down to anything."

"Lovely buckwheat, please close your leaves and lower your flowers," begged the old willow tree. "And whatever you do, do not look at the lightning when it strikes. When the skies split open it gives us a little glimpse into heaven – but it is so dazzling that even humans shouldn't gaze at it. It blinds them, so whatever would it do to us lesser beings?"

"Lesser beings, indeed!" snorted the buckwheat.

"Of course we're good enough to look into heaven!" And boldly all the buckwheat looked straight up, while the lightning blazed across the sky as if the whole world were in flames.

When the terrifying storm had died away, the wildflowers and the corn gently raised their drooping heads. The air was still and pure to breathe, and they felt quite refreshed by the rain. However, the buckwheat was a sorry sight. The plants were scorched black by the lightning and lay limply across the earth.

The old willow tree waved its branches in the wind and large drops of water fell from his green leaves, just as if he were weeping.

"Why do you cry," asked the sparrows, "when everything else is cheerful? Look, the sun is smiling and the clouds are floating in the blue. Can't you smell the scent of growing things? Tell us why you are weeping."

Then the willow told the sparrows why the buckwheat had met its sad end – that the lightning had punished it for its pride.

And this is the tale that the sparrows told me, in turn, when I asked them for a story...